THE FOOTBALL TRIALS

GAME CHANGER

BLOOMSBURY EDUCATION
Bloomsbury Publishing Plc
50 Bedford Square, London, WC1B 3DP, UK

BLOOMSBURY, BLOOMSBURY EDUCATION and the Diana logo
are trademarks of Bloomsbury Publishing Plc

First published in Great Britain in 2018 by Bloomsbury Publishing Plc

A catalogue record for this book is available from the British Library

ISBN: PB: 978-1-4729-4419-1; ePDF: 978-1-4729-4420-7; ePub: 978-1-4729-4417-7

2 4 6 8 10 9 7 5 3 1

Cover design by James Fraser Design
Typeset by Integra Software Services Pvt. Ltd.

Printed and bound in China by Leo Paper Products

To find out more about our authors and books visit www.bloomsbury.com
and sign up for our newsletters

recommended by

www.catchup.org

Catch Up is a charity which aims to address the problem of underachievement
that has its roots in literacy and numeracy difficulties

THE
FOOTBALL TRIALS
GAME
CHANGER

JOHN HICKMAN
Illustrated by NEIL EVANS

BLOOMSBURY EDUCATION

LONDON OXFORD NEW YORK NEW DELHI SYDNEY

CONTENTS

Stepping Up

I still can't believe I'm playing for the under-eighteens. OK, it's only one game, and I'm on the bench, but this is a proper step up. And I can see it's a step up too, as I watch from the sidelines. The players out on the pitch are bigger than me – most of them are a couple of years older.

There are more people watching too. More pressure. Six months ago, I was playing football in the park with my mates. Now I play for United, the biggest team in the world.

And I'm freezing. It's the end of November and if I get out there on the pitch, I'm keeping my gloves on. I don't care whether Granddad thinks "real footballers don't wear gloves," I don't want my fingers to fall off with frostbite. It's probably not even worth thinking about anyway. I bet I don't get to play. Liam, the manager, has just got me on the bench to see what it's like with the under-eighteens.

Why would he bring me on when he has got all these older lads, with loads more experience? Not that I'm moaning – it's great being here. I'm just being realistic.

Right before half time, City score. It's a scrappy goal, the ball bouncing around in our area like a pinball, before their forward toe pokes it past our keeper. Then the ref blows the whistle for half-time.

When the lads get off the pitch, Liam shouts at us. "That's the worst time to concede, right before half-time. You switched off, lads, you can't do that." Liam looks angry most of the time – but now his face is even redder than usual.

I look around at the other lads in the changing room. Some are listening to Liam. Some are looking down at the floor. Everyone is gutted about letting in a goal.

"Jackson," says Liam. "Get your jacket off."

My heart stops. "Me?"

"Think you could do a job on the right?" he asks.

"Right wing?"

"Yeah," he says. "Up to it?"

Up to it? I would play anywhere he wanted me too. Stick me in goal, I don't care! "Yeah," I tell him, trying to keep it cool. "I'm up to it."

The second half kicks off and my first touch is loose. The ball bounces off me like I'm made of rubber. I knew this was a bad idea.

I'm not ready for this level. Liam should have left me on the bench, where I was safe, where I wouldn't have made an idiot of myself. He's never going to pick me for the under-eighteens again.

But this is my chance. If I play well here, who knows what can happen? I need to focus. Be confident. I can do this.

My second touch is better, but their left back gets his foot in straight away, knocking the ball out. As the half goes on, I warm up, even though I'm absolutely freezing. I knock the ball about, make a few nice passes.

Then I get the ball out on the right, run at their left back. One step-over, then another. He doesn't know what day it is. I stop the ball. He stops. I go forward, making a bit of space. I whip a cross in.

Bang. Our forward, Anton, gets his head on it. Right into the top corner. Their keeper doesn't stand a chance.

Some of the lads rush to Anton, some race over to me. Anton points at me as he celebrates, and runs over, wrapping his arm around me. I'm buzzing!

My second assist is even better. I get the ball in midfield and chip it over their defence. Our left-winger takes it on the chest, outpaces their back line and slots it past the keeper. The whistle blows and we win, 2–1. Our players come over and give me a pat on the back or a fist-bump. Even the City players tell me I played well.

Liam throws his arm around me as we walk off the pitch. "Well played, Jax. If you keep making that step up, you'll get that pro contract," he says. "Just keep your head down, keep working, and you could go all the way."

I can feel the smile on my face.

Liam goes to talk to some parents. Wheeler, my best mate, and my girlfriend, Lauren, jog over.

"Well played man," says Wheeler.

"You were awesome," says Lauren. "Wasn't he?"

"Mate," says Wheeler, "you should see what people are saying on online." He pulls his phone out, and reads someone's post to me: "If Jackson Law doesn't make the United first team, there's something not right with the world."

"Nice one," I say.

"Nice one? It's amazing! There's loads like that," he tells me. "Everyone is raving about you."

I'm totally buzzing. It's a shame Mum and Granddad aren't here. Granddad has been poorly these last few weeks, so Mum stayed at home with him.

I walk Lauren back to her place, then head home myself. All the way back it's on my mind. A pro contract. I've been saving most of my wages each week, and I've got about £5,000. I haven't told Mum or Granddad, but I'm saving up for somewhere nice to live, somewhere much nicer than the tower block where we live now. If I got a pro contract, I would be able to buy an amazing place!

Then I see someone sitting on the wall, at the end of the alley. I grab my phone, and hold onto it. People get robbed around here, sometimes.

As I get closer, the person stands up. My heart thumps. Something is about to go off. This is all I need.

Then the person speaks. "Jackson?" It's a man's voice. And I know who it is straight away, even though I haven't heard that voice in nine years.

It's my dad.

Dad

I was shocked to get a call-up to the under-eighteens, but seeing my dad, after all these years – this is the biggest shock of them all. He has a shaved head, a beard, and a thick gold chain around his neck.

"Alright?" he says. His hands are in the pockets of a leather jacket that looks too big for him. He gives me a smile, but it's like he doesn't really want to be smiling at all. He's bent over, like he's ashamed. I had an idea in my head of what my dad would be like now. I thought he would be big, strong, someone you wouldn't mess around with. But he's the exact opposite. Skinny, weak, and he looks like someone people walk all over. I don't know why, but I feel guilty. I feel bad for him. Surely it should be the other way around?

"How have you been keeping?" he asks, and I don't answer. "It has been a while," he says, and I think, "yeah, it has been nine years and you haven't come anywhere near me."

"I heard about United," my dad says. "You're playing for the youth team. Is that right?"

"Yeah," I tell him.

"Wow!" he says. "My boy playing for United? I'm made-up for you, I really am. Your mum must be so proud."

I think about Mum and how she has brought me up on her own, pretty much most of my life, and how Dad walked out on us. I just stare at him.

"I know you probably don't want to talk to me," he says. "But I've always asked around to find out how you were doing."

I think about asking him why I never got a birthday card or Christmas present. But I don't. I keep my mouth shut and just squeeze my hands into fists.

"So I knew you and your mum still lived round here," he says. "I thought if I hung around long enough, you would turn up. How is she anyway? Your mum?"

"She's fine," I tell him.

"Good," he says. "Glad to hear it. I know she will have told you lots of things about me, but I would like to tell you my side of things," he says. "Some time, maybe?"

I just look at him.

"Anyway," he says. "If you ever want a chat, I'm in The Unicorn most days. It's not far."

That makes sense. I can smell the beer on him.

"Nice seeing you," he says. He gives me another sad smile and walks away. I just stand there, thinking about what has just happened.

When I get home, I think about not telling Mum and Granddad about meeting Dad, but that seems wrong.

Mum doesn't take it well. "If he bothers you again, you tell me, OK?" she says. "He is probably only hanging around because he has heard about United, and thinks there will be money in it for him. That man is bad news."

"Yes," says Granddad. "But he's also the boy's dad. Go easy."

"OK," says Mum. "But promise me, if your dad bothers you again, you will tell me."

I nod, and I wish I hadn't told them anything about seeing my dad.

The Unicorn

The next day after school, me and Wheeler have a kick about in the park. We knock the ball back and forward to one another.

"Wheels, can I ask you something," I say. "About my old man?"

"Yeah?"

"I saw him yesterday. He was hanging about outside the flat."

"Hanging about?" he asks.

"Waiting for me," I say. "He wanted to talk."

"When did you see him last?" he asks.

"Dunno," I say, even though I do know. "When I was like seven or something."

"That's a long time," he says.

"He said he wants to talk to me, to explain his side of things. Do you think I should meet him?" I ask.

"Of course you should," says Wheeler. "He's your dad."

I was hoping he would say that.

An hour later, me and Wheeler are standing outside The Unicorn, a run-down old man's pub about fifteen minutes from my flat. It's mad to think I never knew where my dad was all this time, and he has only been a quarter of an hour away.

"Go on then," says Wheeler.

I take a breath and step inside the pub.

For once, my dad wasn't lying. He is standing at the bar, in that same leather coat, with a pint of beer in his hand.

I can feel my heart banging as I walk over.

"Alright, Dad?" I say.

Then he turns around, sees me. At first he looks shocked, then a big smile fills his face.

"Jackson, how's it going? Good to see you," he says. "Lads," he says to some other men at the bar, "this is my boy, Jackson."

They all nod at me.

"Gentlemen, you're looking at the next Jesse Walters right here," my dad tells the other men. "Jackson plays for United, don't you, son?"

I smile, feeling awkward.

My dad looks at Wheeler. "I know you," he says. "What's your name again?"

"Scott," says Wheeler. "But everyone just calls me Wheeler."

"I thought I knew your face. You used to be best mates with Jackson when you were little."

"We still are," I say.

"It's good to have a best mate," says Dad. "Let me get you both a drink."

He orders us both a cola and we take a seat away from the bar, near the pool table.

"I used to bring you here when you were little, to have a game of pool," says Dad."

I remember, but I don't say anything.

"Anyway, boys," says Dad. "I just need to make a quick phone call. I won't be a minute." He gets up and goes off.

"He seems alright," says Wheeler.

"Yeah," I say. And I think about being a kid, playing pool with my dad. I realise how much I've missed him.

When Dad comes back, we talk about old times, about how we used to watch the football together, how we would play over at the park, how he got me into United. "I'm telling you," says Dad, "you definitely get your skills from me. I could probably have signed for United myself."

"Why didn't you?" asks Wheeler.

Dad lifts his pint up. "This stuff," he says. "And women." He winks at me.

Then someone shouts out: "Ash."

My dad turns.

A big guy who everyone calls Smiley is standing near the pub door. Smiley is definitely not very smiley. He is, however, not the sort of guy you mess with. "I want a word with you," he says to my dad.

Dad looks scared. "I won't be a minute," he says. He jumps up and rushes out after Smiley. I look at Wheeler and ask: "Is he in trouble?"

Smiley

Everybody has heard of Smiley. He's a
real trouble-maker. He's big, built like a tank.
You can tell he works out all day – his biceps
are massive. He always wears a parka and
he has a tattoo of a teardrop under his eye.

Smiley is dangerous – and I want to know what he wants with my dad.

We sneak to the window and watch Smiley have a go at Dad on the car park. I can't hear what they're saying, but I can tell it's not good.

"People say Smiley keeps a gun under his bed," whispers Wheeler.

"Don't tell me that," I whisper back.

"Just saying," says Wheeler.

Then, we see Smiley thump my dad in the gut. My dad doubles over and I feel like someone has punched me in the belly too. I watch Smiley point at my dad, shout something, then walk away. My dad walks slowly back to the pub.

Me and Wheeler hurry away from the window, back to our table.

After a moment, Dad sits at the table too, rubbing his gut. He doesn't look me or Wheeler in the eye. It's like he's ashamed, just like he was when I saw him the other night.

"You OK?" I ask.

"Yeah, yeah," he says. "Just a bit of business."

I look across at Wheeler, and he just shakes his head.

"I wasn't spying or anything," I say. "But we saw what happened."

"Nothing happened," says Dad.

"We saw him thump you," I tell him.

Dad looks at me a moment, then looks away.

"What does Smiley want with you?" I ask.

"You don't need to know," he tells me.

"I want to know."

Dad takes a drink from his pint. "I owe him some money. A lot of money. Nothing for you to worry about," he says.

"Yeah, right," I tell him.

Life Savings

The next day at football training, I can't control the ball properly, I can't pick out a pass. Nothing I do works out. I keep thinking about Smiley thumping my dad. It's like he has thumped me. And I can't stop thinking about that gun under Smiley's bed, and what might happen if my dad doesn't pay up.

After training, Liam takes me to one side.

"Everything alright?" he asks.

"Yeah, fine," I tell him.

"It doesn't seem like it," he says.

"Just Granddad," I lie. "He has not been too well lately."

"I thought I hadn't seen him for a bit," says Liam. "If there's anything I can do, just let me know."

"Thanks," I say.

After training, I go to the bank. I can't draw all of my money out of the cash-point, there's too much. So I have to go inside.
The woman behind the counter frowns at me when I ask for £5,000, and asks me for ID.
I show it to her and she doesn't say anything.
Outside, I stuff the wedge of money into my backpack.

* * *

In The Unicorn, Dad is at the bar again, just like he was a few days ago. "Alright, Dad," I say.

"Alright, mate," he says. "What you doing here?"

"Can I have a word?" I ask.

He sits down at a table with me. "What's up?" he asks me.

I unzip my backpack, and pull out a thick wad of notes.

"What's all that?" he asks.

"Money," I tell him.

"I can see that," he says. "What are you doing with it?"

I offer it to him, but he doesn't take it.

"There's five grand," I tell him. "Take it."

"For what?"

"To pay off Smiley."

"I can't take your money," he says. "Where did you get it?"

"It's my savings," I tell him.

"All of it?" he asks.

I nod.

"Thought footballers earned millions these days," he says.

"One day," I tell him. "Maybe."

"I can't take it," he says. "It's not right."

"Please," I say. "Is it enough?"

"It's a good start," he says. "I don't know what to say."

"No big deal," I tell him. I think about that house I wanted to help Mum and Granddad get, but push the thought out of my head.

"I'll pay you back, every penny," he says.

"OK."

"I'm not joking, Jackson, I mean it," he says. "Tell you what, when are you playing next? Would it be alright if I came along and watched?"

Pain

The following Saturday, I'm on the bench for the under-eighteen match against Rovers. I might have started if I had been on my game in training. Wheeler and Lauren watch from the sidelines again. But there is no sign of my dad. I'm gutted. Worst of all, I talked Mum out of coming along, and told her to stay with Granddad, because I was worried what might happen if Dad rocked up and Mum was here.

When I finally get on, I'm useless. My tackling is terrible. My passing is poor. My shooting is shocking. My head is just not in the game at all.

All I can think about is Dad and him letting me down all over again.

We are 1–0 down and the game is almost over. Then the ball comes to me on the edge of the box. I struggle to get it under control, but I do. I knock it to my right, get a clear sight of goal.

Jamal is screaming at me to pass it.

Even though I've been rubbish all half, this is my chance to put things right.

I have to take it.

I hit the ball hard.

It flies over the bar. Nowhere near. I just stand there, hands on my hips, feeling like a complete loser.

"Effort," says a Rovers defender sarcastically.

Jamal stares at me, shakes his head. "I was open, man," he says. "You should have passed it."

My head drops.

The ref blows his whistle.

Game over.

At home that night, while Mum is making tea, Granddad watches the same cowboy movie he watches every week. He moves in his seat and groans.

"Are you OK?" I ask.

"Fine," he says.

"Doesn't sound like it," I tell him.

"Never mind me," he says. "It's you I'm worried about."

"I'm all good," I tell him.

"Come off it," he says. "You've not been yourself since last week, when your dad showed up."

Just hearing the word "dad" feels like a punch in my guts.

"I have," I lie.

"Come on, Jackson," he says. "It's me you're talking to. I'm not daft."

"Are you sure about that?" I joke.

"Well I might be a bit daft, but I know when something is up with you. Have you seen him again?"

I think about lying. "It's alright," says Granddad. "I won't say anything."

"I'm sorry," I say.

"There's nothing to be sorry for," he tells me. "He's your dad, of course you want to see him. I've told your mum that, but she doesn't get it, she thinks it's simple."

"It's not," I tell him.

"I know it's not," he says. "I've held my tongue about your dad. It's not really my place to say anything, but this is what I think. He was a selfish toe-rag who put himself first. He might have changed. I like to believe people can change – I mean I was no angel growing up – but you need to be careful."

"Yeah," I say, and I'm already starting to think that giving Dad all my money was a bad idea.

"But you're a good lad," says Granddad. "You're old enough and bright enough to make your own choices, your own mistakes. Are you planning on seeing him again?"

I shake my head. "I don't know."

Betrayal

That night after tea, I head out, telling Mum and Granddad I'm going round to Wheeler's place. It's not a complete lie. I do go to Wheeler's, but we don't stay there. Instead, the two of us ride our bikes over to The Unicorn.

I don't want my money back – all I want to know is why my dad didn't turn up at my match, when he promised he would.

At The Unicorn, I see my dad outside the entrance, smoking.

There's someone else with him.

Smiley.

The two of them are laughing and joking like they're best mates. I grab Wheeler, pull him back. We hide around the corner and listen.

"What are you doing?" asks Wheeler.

"My dad," I tell him. "He's with Smiley."

Wheeler looks around the corner, watches them chatting. I watch them too.

"No way," whispers Wheeler. "I thought they hated each other."

I listen in on their conversation.

"So do you think I should try and chat up that new barmaid?" asks Smiley.

"Why not?" says Dad. "What have you got to lose?"

"My pride?"

"I know all about that," says Dad.

Smiley takes a long pull on his cigarette and flicks it onto the ground. "So do you feel bad then or what?" he asks.

"About what?" asks Dad.

"Scamming your boy."

"The kid will be loaded in a couple of years," says Dad. "He won't miss a few grand."

"Well, I'm happy to give you a smack any time," says Smiley. "So long as I get my share of the money."

"Maybe go a bit easier next time?" says Dad.

Smiley laughs. Dad finishes his cigarette and they go back into the pub.

I feel so angry. How could I be so stupid? How could I let him use me like that?

"Are you OK?" asks Wheeler.

"Yeah, man," I lie.

"I can't believe he has done that," Wheeler says.

"I can," I tell him. I lift my bike up, turn it around.

"Where are you going?" asks Wheeler.

"Home," I tell him.

"No way," he says. "We are getting that money back."

"Yeah?" I say. "And how are we going to do that?"

The Old Man

Instead of going home, me and Wheeler wait outside The Unicorn, sitting on some bollards at the edge of the car park, out of sight of the entrance. I ring Mum, tell her I'm staying at Wheeler's, and we wait in the car park until my dad leaves the pub.

When he does come out, at half eleven, we follow him to a scruffy little house five minutes from The Unicorn, on this scruffy little estate. I make a note of the address in my phone.

I stay at Wheeler's that night. The next day, we get up bright and early. We head back to my dad's estate, and hang about not far from his place. We wait there a couple of hours, kicking our ball about.

Then I see Dad leave his house.

I grab my ball and we hide, watching him go. He walks off down the street, and we wait behind the wall, until he is out of sight.

"Come on," says Wheeler.

He leads the way, over to my dad's place. He has a look up and down the street, before pushing the gate open.

I have another look up and down before I follow him. I watch Wheeler as he tries the gate at the side of the house. It's locked.

Then Wheeler climbs over the fence. I listen as he unbolts the gate on the other side, opens it.

"You really think this is a good idea?" I ask.

"Just come on," he says.

I take another look around, then go through the gate, which Wheeler closes behind me.

The back yard is a dump, filled with long grass, like some mini jungle.

Wheeler tries the back door. It's locked. But there's a small window which has been left open, which Wheeler pulls open wider.

"You won't fit," I tell him.

"Watch me." He jumps up and squeezes in through the window, like a giant worm.

He wriggles all the way inside, pulling his boots through last. I look around, checking whether anyone is watching, but the garden has tall fences on each side and massive trees at the back.

I can see the dark shape of Wheeler through the window in the back door. See him messing with the bolts, turning the key.

The back door opens and I go inside.

Inside, the place is dark. The kitchen is manky – full of empty cans and wine bottles.

In the living room, Wheeler looks all around for the money.

I pull open a drawer in the sideboard. It's filled with letters and medicine pots, but I can't find the money. When I see the state of this place, I feel bad for my dad. I'm not sure I even want my money back.

"What if he has put the money in the bank?" I ask.

"He won't have done that," says Wheeler.

"Or maybe he has spent it all," I say.

"You can't spend £5,000 in a few days," says Wheeler. "There has to be some left."

Once we have searched the living room, we check upstairs. I search through some drawers in a little bedroom. It must be my dad's room. The walls are covered in old United mirrors.

"Jax!" whispers Wheeler. "Here."

He must have found some of the money. I hurry out of the room and into another bedroom. Wheeler is just standing there.

But there's no money in his hands.

He points to the bed.

There is an old guy asleep in the bed. He is black and skinny, and looks really sick.

I don't know what to think.

Then I hear the front door open.

Dad is back.

Captured

Wheeler and I hide in Dad's bedroom, behind the door. I'm so nervous; I can hear my heart thumping in my ears.

I can hear footsteps on the stairs.

Then he's on the landing, outside the bedroom.

My heart stops.

He walks past, into the other room, where the old man was sleeping.

I can hear the sound of someone opening a plastic bag, and the crack of a can being opened.

I want to know what is going on – who that old man is, what my dad is doing with him. Even though I'm scared, I creep out of the room, onto the landing.

"How are you feeling this morning, Pop?" asks Dad.

The old man groans.

"Well don't worry, I'm here," says Dad. "I told you I wouldn't leave, didn't I? I won't let you down."

I decide I need some answers, so I step into the old man's bedroom.

Dad sees me, and nearly falls backwards. "Jackson, what are you doing here?"

"Why did you lie to me?" I ask.

"About what?" he says. "What are you on about?"

"You scammed me," I tell him. "I heard you, with Smiley."

"No," he says. "You've got it wrong."

"I heard you," I tell him.

Then Wheeler steps into the room. "We both heard you," he says. "Don't lie."

Dad sees Wheeler. "How did you get in here? What are you playing at?"

"Why did you lie to me?" I ask again.

"Alright, alright," he says. "Not in here. Let's leave him in peace." He leads us out onto the landing, closing the bedroom door behind him.

"So," I say. "Why did you lie?"

"I needed the money," he says. "I was desperate."

"So desperate you would rip off your own son?" asks Wheeler.

"I'm not proud," says Dad. "But I had to do something. It's Pop," he goes on. "The old fella in there. Your granddad, Jackson."

I feel hot and sick. "My granddad?" I ask.

"He's not well. I've been staying at home to look after him, haven't been able to work or anything. Run up my own debts too, drinking and that, my own fault. Looks like we might lose the house. When I heard about you with United, I thought you would be minted – I didn't realise you would give me all your savings."

A jumble of feelings whirls around inside me. I hate that my dad lied and ripped me off, but I sort of understand. I would do anything I could to keep a roof over Granddad – my other granddad – and Mum's head.

"But why did you lie?" I ask him. "You could have just told me the truth."

"I don't know," he says. "I didn't want you to feel sorry for us, I guess. I was embarrassed."

"And how do I know you're not lying to me now?" I ask.

"I'm not," he tells me. "I swear to you."

He sounds like he is telling the truth, but I thought that when he told me about Smiley. I can't believe anything he says. "Just keep the money," I tell him, and I feel like I might cry. "Come on, Wheeler."

I go to leave, but Dad grabs a hold of my shoulder. "I didn't want to leave you and your mum. But I had to. I knew I would drag you both down, sooner or later."

I hurry down the stairs. Wheeler is close behind me. My eyes sting and my stomach hurts as I slam the front door behind us.

A United Player

A week or so later, I'm back on the bench for our under-sixteen game. Hopefully I'll be back in the under-eighteens soon. I'll just have to do what Liam told me, keep my head down and work hard. As the lads are playing out on the pitch, I look up and down the line.

I'm looking for my dad, even though I know there's no chance he'll have come. Lauren and my mum are there and I wonder why I even bothered with Dad. I don't need anyone else. I've got all the support and love I need.

"Jax," says Liam, "get your jacket off."

I pull my jacket off quickly and when the substitution is made I'm buzzing to be out on the pitch.

Ollie passes the ball to me and I take it sweetly. I knock a long pass across the pitch, which Jamal takes on his chest.

"Ball," says Ollie.

Jamal has a shot, but the keeper saves it and suddenly they're attacking us.

I slide in, win the ball back and I'm running with the ball. I dribble past one, then two. Step-over with my right. Then my left. Right again. I turn one way, and a defender slides in. I go the other, leaving him on his backside.

I shape myself, ready to shoot.

For a moment, I imagine missing, the ball flying up into the sky.

But I push that to one side. All of it.

Then I hit the ball with the inside of my right foot. It bends into the top corner. An absolute screamer.

Everyone crowds around me. Ryan jumps up on my shoulders.

Ollie hugs me.

"Good to have you back," he says.

"Good to be back," I tell him.

I make a promise to myself. No matter what happens, no one or nothing is going to stop me from doing this. Not my dad, not anyone.

I'm going to be a United player.

Bonus Bits!

Quiz Time

Find out how good your knowledge of the story is by answering these multiple choice questions. There are answers at the end (but no peeking before you finish!).

1. Why does Jackson most want a pro contract?

A to help his granddad get treatment

B to buy a fast car for himself

C to buy a nice house for his family

D to show he is the best at football

2. Why does Mum think Dad is getting in touch now?

A he heard about Jackson playing for United and wants money

B he wants to upset Jackson's mum by telling Jackson the truth

C he wants to apologise and have a good relationship with Jackson

D he wants to help Granddad get better

3. Why does Jackson's father say Smiley has thumped him?

   A he is a mean person

   B he has hit Smiley before

   C he owes Smiley money

   D he owes Smiley a weapon

4. How does Wheeler get in to Jackson's dad's house?

   A through a large window

   B through a small window

   C through the back door

   D through the front door

5. What do they find in the house that surprises them?

   A a football contract

   B lots of money

   C stolen goods

   D a man asleep in bed

6. What made Jackson's football skills not as good as usual?

   A he was playing with better players

   B worries about stealing money

   C worries about his Dad

   D he had hurt his foot at the pub

Working Out Words

Here are the definitions for some of the trickier words in this book.

realistic: having a sensible idea of what can be achieved or expected.
"Why would he bring me on when he has got all these older lads, with loads more experience? Not that I'm moaning – it's great being here. I'm just being realistic."

frostbite: an injury to the body that is caused by extremely cold conditions. It usually affects the nose, fingers or toes.
"I don't want my fingers to fall off with frostbite."

pinball: a game where small metal balls are fired across a sloping board to score points when they hit certain targets.

"It's a scrappy goal, the ball bouncing around in our area like a pinball, before their forward toe pokes it past our keeper."

concede (a goal): when your team fails to stop the other team from scoring a goal.

"When the lads get off the pitch, Liam shouts at us. 'That's the worst time to concede, right before half-time.'"

an assist: in football when a player helps to score a goal, e.g. by passing the ball to an attacker who actually puts the ball in the net.

"My second assist is even better. I get the ball in midfield and chip it over their defence."

parka: a large warm jacket with a hood.

"He always wears a parka and he has a tattoo of a teardrop under his eye."

minted: having a lot of money which makes you rich.

"When I heard about you with United, I thought you would be minted"

WHAT NEXT?

There are lots of emotional decisions Jackson has to make in this story. How would you feel if you were Jackson?

- How would you feel towards Dad when he was punched by Smiley?
- How would you feel when you heard Dad talking to Smiley about the money?
- How do you feel towards Dad at the end of the story?

ANSWERS 3to QUIZ TIME

1B, 2A, 3C, 4B, 5D, 6C

Look out for all of Jackson's adventures!

978-1-4729-4411-5

978-1-4729-4415-3

978-1-4729-4419-1

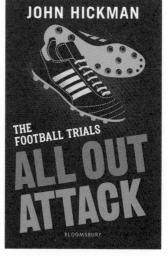

978-1-4729-4423-8